THE BIG BIRTHDAY SURPRISE

Junior Discovers Giving

by **Dave Ramsey**

Collect all of the *Junior's Adventures* books!

For more information on Dave Ramsey, visit daveramsey.com or call 888.227.3223.

Editors: Amy Parker, Jen Gingerich
Project Management: Preston Cannon, Bryan Amerine and Mallory Darcy
Illustrations: Greg Hardin, John Trent and Kenny Yamada
Art Direction: Luke LeFevre, Brad Dennison and Chris Carrico

DEDICATION

Daniel is our youngest child and our only boy.
He has learned a lot from his sisters. They taught
him quickly not to have a grocery store fit!

Thank you, Daniel, for having an open heart that
is willing to learn life principles from your family.
And thank you for having such a tender spirit . . .
always thinking of others.

Love, Dad (Dave)

Junior ran into the kitchen
    and did a sock-slide past the fridge.

Looking at the calendar, he announced,
    "Only five more days till my birthday!"

Mrow.

Scout was not impressed.

As Junior bounced on the bus, he thought of all
of the gifts that he would get for his birthday.

He'd asked for a scooter. And an army man.
A video game . . . and a *real* guitar.
Oh, and a drum set.

That was all.

He could
hardly wait.

"Okay, class," Ms. Harper began. "This week is our food drive for the children's home. We're asking each student to bring in three food items. Then, at the end of the week, I'll choose two of you to help me deliver it."

Emma raised her hand. "Why don't the kids have food?"

"Well, they do right now. But these children don't have moms and dads to take care of them, so every year we try to help by giving the home something that the children can use."

"Mom," he said before taking his first bite, "may I have a can of corn, a can of peas, and two boxes of mac 'n' cheese?"

Mom looked at Junior's full plate and scrunched her brow.

"It's for the kids at the children's home," he explained. "We're collecting food at school."

"Oh, Junior." Mom stood up and wrapped him in a hug. "Of course! Take as much as you want."

Junior gulped. He wasn't so sure that he wanted to go meet these kids without moms and dads.

What would they look like? What would they talk about? What would they do?

Junior carried a box of food and slowly followed
Ms. Harper and Emma up the steps to the big
house. Before Ms. Harper could even knock, a
smiling woman opened the door. A dozen laughing
kids quickly surrounded them.

"Mac 'n' cheese! My favorite!" A boy about Junior's age reached for the box. "Here, I'll take that to the kitchen. I'm Chris. What's your name?"

"I—I'm Junior," Junior answered, following Chris to the kitchen.

After putting the food away, the boys headed outside.

"Wanna play catch?" Junior asked.

"Well, I don't have a baseball glove," Chris answered, "but do you like to climb trees?" He bounded up a tree and swung from the limb.

"Cool!" Junior was right behind him.

They played and played until Ms. Harper called Junior to go.

That night, as Junior was settling into bed, his mom stopped by his room. "Good night, sweetie. Big day tomorrow!"

Junior had almost forgotten—the party! Junior grinned back at her. He knew how hard she had worked on the party. And she had invited just about every kid he knew!

But as Junior tried to fall asleep, he just kept thinking about one kid: Chris. He was the only boy Junior knew who didn't have a baseball glove.

The next morning was a blur of streamers and balloons and presents. In no time, Junior was holding the last gift in his hand. It was a plain, white envelope, but from the look on Grandma's face, Junior knew it had to be good.

He carefully pulled the flap open and looked inside. "Whooaaaa!" Junior ran to his grandmother, clutching the crisp hundred-dollar bill. "Thanks, Grandma! Thanks a hundred!"

"Spend it wisely," she answered with a wink.

When the last guest left—before the door had even closed—Junior turned to his dad. "Hey, Dad, will you drive me to the store?"

"Is that hundred-dollar bill already burning a hole in your pocket?" Dad laughed. "Let me help clean up some of this first. Then we can go."

"Thanks, Dad!" Junior yelled, halfway up the stairs.

"V

"After we go to the store, could we take these to the children's home? I think they could use them."

"Of course," Dad answered. Mom's face wrinkled into a weird smile, and her eyes welled up with tears. Dad spoke for both of them. "That is such a thoughtful thing to do, Junior. We're so proud of you."

At the children's home that afternoon,
the kids were so excited about all of the toys.

Junior looked around for his new friend.
He finally spotted Chris walking toward him.

"Hey, Junior! Thank you for all the toys!
You want to play a game of checkers?"

"Well," Junior said, pulling a gift from out of his backpack, "I thought you might like to play with this instead."

Chris's eyes grew wide as he unwrapped a brand-new baseball and glove.

Junior grinned. "Wanna play catch?"

"Are you kidding me?" Chris answered. He ran for the door with Junior right behind him.

"Thanks, Dad," Junior said as they rode home that night.
"That was the best birthday ever."

And they both knew that the **best** birthday present was the one Junior gave away.